Little Mole Finds Hope

For my Mona, in celebration of new life. I love you, Mum.
—G.N.

26 25 24 23 22 21 20   1 2 3 4 5 6 7 8

ISBN: 9781506448749

Written by Glenys Nellist
Illustrated by Sally Garland

Library of Congress Cataloging-in-Publication Data

Names: Nellist, Glenys, 1959- author. | Garland, Sally Anne, illustrator.
Title: Little Mole finds hope / by Glenys Nellist ; illustrated by Sally
  Garland.
Description: Minneapolis, MN : Beaming Books, [2020] | Audience: Ages 5-8.
  | Summary: Little Mole is sad, so his mother teaches him about hope by
  leading the way out of their dark burrow into a bright world filled with
  the promise of spring.
Identifiers: LCCN 2019034530 | ISBN 9781506448749 (hardcover)
Subjects: CYAC: Hope--Fiction. | Sadness--Fiction. | Moles
  (Animals)--Fiction.
Classification: LCC PZ7.1.N433 Lit 2020 | DDC [E]--dc23
LC record available at https://lccn.loc.gov/2019034530

VN0004589; 9781506448749; DEC2019

Beaming Books
510 Marquette Avenue
Minneapolis, MN 55402

Beamingbooks.com

Little Mole Finds Hope

by Glenys Nellist
illustrated by Sally Garland

beaming books
MINNEAPOLIS

Little Mole was sad.

He lay in his burrow, deep underground,
and put his head in his paws.

"Little Mole, whatever's wrong?" asked Mama.

"I just don't know, Mama," sniffed Little Mole.
"But I don't feel good inside. I'm sad."

"What you need is hope," Mama said.

"Hope? What's hope? Where do I find it?"
Little Mole asked.

"Come with me," Mama said, as she took hold
of Little Mole's paw. "Sometimes, hope is hiding
in the darkness. Sometimes it's hard to see.
But it's always there. You just have to find it."

Mama led her son gently
out of the dark burrow,
up toward the light.
But on their way out
of the tunnel, Mama stopped.

"No, my dear," Mama whispered softly. "This bulb is not dead. Sometime soon, it will feel the warmth of the sun. It will begin to grow and push its way out of the deep, cold earth. One day, this bulb will become a beautiful yellow daffodil."

"Close your eyes, Little Mole. Can you see it dancing in the wind?"

"Yes, Mama!" cried Little Mole. "I see it! I see it!"

"*That* is hope," Mama said.

Little Mole and Mama reached the top of the burrow, where the sun was shining.

"Look up, Little Mole," Mama said. "What do you see?"

Little Mole looked up. He saw woodpeckers sitting in the trees. But the branches were bare. They stretched out like skeleton bones silhouetted against the sky.

"They're dead, Mama," said Little Mole.

"No, my dear," Mama whispered softly. "The trees are not dead. One day soon, buds will appear, and these branches will be covered in bright green leaves."

"Close your eyes, Little Mole. Can you see them dancing in the wind?"

"Yes, Mama!" cried Little Mole. "I see them! I see them!"

"*That* is hope," Mama said.

Little Mole and his mama
scurried along the edge
of the woods until they
came to Mr. Rabbit's garden.

An old brown flowerpot was lying on its side in the soil. Under the rim, something small and shriveled was hanging.

"It's dead, Mama," said Little Mole.

"No, my dear," Mama whispered softly.

"This chrysalis is not dead. One day soon, the butterfly growing inside will burst out of her shell."

"She will spread her wings and fly free among the flowers. Close your eyes, Little Mole," said Mama.

"Can you see her dancing in the wind?"

"Yes, Mama!" cried Little Mole. "I see her! I see her!"

"*That* is hope," Mama said.

Little Mole and his mama went home.

"I had a wonderful day today, Mama."
Little Mole said happily. "Now I know
that there's always hope, even in the
darkest places."

Mama smiled as she tucked Little Mole into bed, pulled his quilt up under his chin, and kissed him good night.

And Little Mole closed his eyes and fell fast asleep,
dreaming of yellow daffodils, green trees, and
beautiful butterflies dancing together in the wind.

Discussion Guide for Caregivers

DID YOU KNOW ...

Moles have little rooms in their underground tunnels. They have a special room where baby moles are born, bedrooms, and even a kitchen where they store earthworms—their favorite food!

TALK ABOUT THE STORY

- Why do you think Little Mole might have been sad? When have you felt sad?

- What three things did Little Mole see when he closed his eyes and used his imagination?

- Close your eyes. Think about something that makes you really happy. See the pictures in your mind. Tell me about it.

- Now it's your turn. Tell your child that you're going to close your eyes and think about something that makes you happy. Let her ask you about it.

TIPS TO HELP A CHILD WHO IS FEELING SAD

Most children will experience sadness. You, the caregiver, are their primary hope-giver.

- Acknowledge how your child is feeling.

- Ask her to talk about, or draw, her feelings. Listen and empathize.

- Reassure your child that his sadness will not last forever.

- Hug your child. Don't stop until your child does.

- Spend time together, doing something enjoyable.

- Teach your child gratitude. Find a way to record 'things that made me smile today'. Use a journal, or a 'gratitude jar' containing slips of paper.

- Adequate sleep, good nutrition, and regular exercise all contribute towards your child's emotional health and well-being.

FINDING HOPE

Finding light amidst darkness and new life springing from what seems dead—are universal symbols of hope. Talk with your child about times you've felt hopeful or experienced new life out of difficult situations. When your family or your child goes through a difficult season, remember Little Mole and how he looked for signs of hope. You can look for signs of hope too.

GLENYS NELLIST is the author of multiple children's books, including the bestselling *'Twas the Evening of Christmas* and the popular series *Love Letters from God* and *Snuggle Time*. Her writing reflects a deep passion for helping children discover joy in the world. Glenys lives in Michigan with her husband, David.

SALLY GARLAND was brought up in a small town in the Highlands of Scotland called Alness and studied illustration at Edinburgh College of Art before moving to Glasgow, where she now lives and works with her partner and young son. Since Sally was young, she has loved drawing and had a passion for children's literature and illustration. Her current influences include vintage picture book illustration from the 1950s and 1960s.